Find
Scrooge
in
A Christmas
Carol

Illustrations
and script development
by Bob Terrio

Illustration assistant: Gale Terrio

Louis Weber, C.E.O.
Publications International, Ltd.
7373 North Cicero Avenue
Lincolnwood, Illinois 60646

Manufactured in the U.S.A.

8 7 6 5 4 3 2 1

ISBN 0-7853-0329-4

PUBLICATIONS INTERNATIONAL, LTD.

BILLINGS COUNTY PUBLIC SCHOOL
Box 307
Medora, North Dakota 58645

"Bah, humbug!" snorts old Ebenezer Scrooge as he hurries down the street. All around him, the people of London are getting into the Christmas spirit, but Scrooge would rather be grumpy all year round. Can you imagine a more gloomy fellow than Ebenezer Scrooge?

Look for Ebenezer Scrooge in this Christmas Eve scene. Then see if you can find these people who *do* have the Christmas spirit.

Scrooge Holly Day Hiram Yule

Timothy Scamp Lady Sarah

Mortimer Nog

Prunella Pudding Mistress Mistletoe

Christmas Eve is nothing special at Scrooge's counting house. Poor Bob Cratchit won't be allowed to leave a minute early tonight. Even Scrooge's nephew, who has stopped by to wish him a Merry Christmas, can't cheer up the old grouch.

This place is a mess because Scrooge can't bear to throw anything out! Look for these things that Scrooge has kept for all these years.

His first penny

His first spectacles

His first shoes

His first top hat

His first inkwell

His first pen

His first change purse

His first clerk

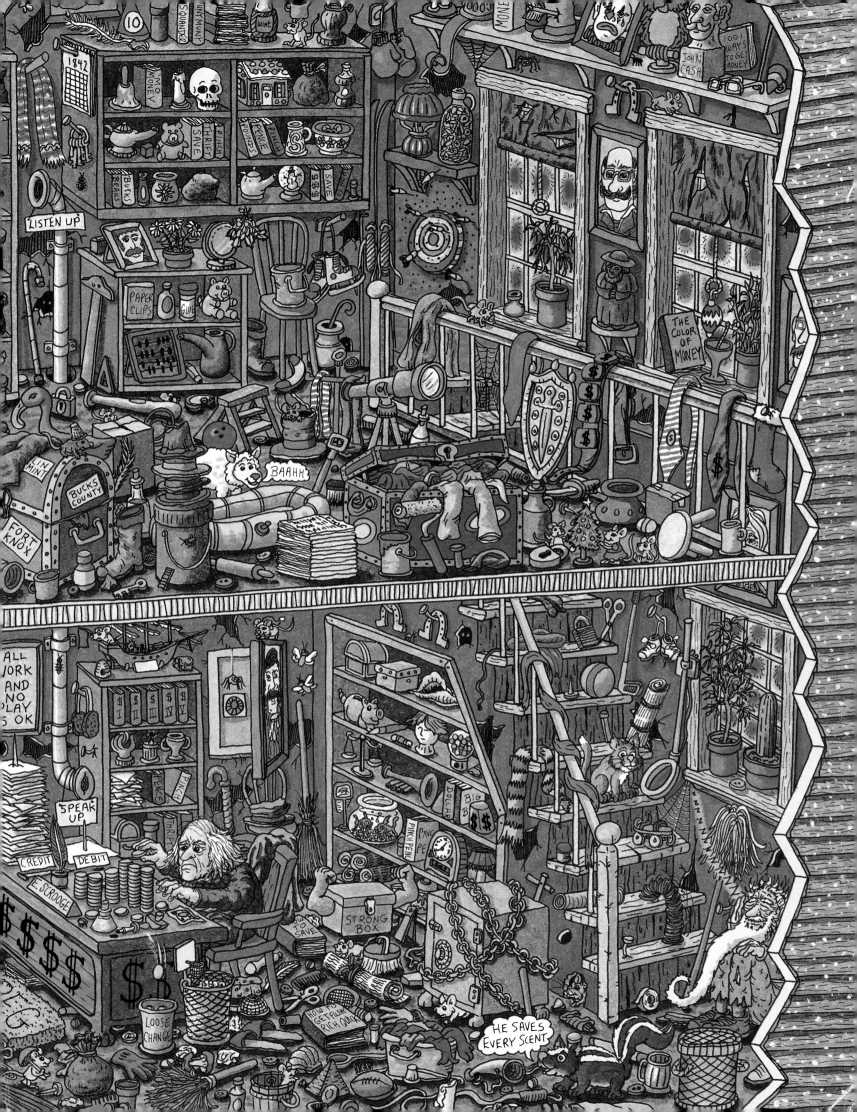

It's almost closing time, but the stores are filled with last-minute shoppers. Ebenezer Scrooge is having his usual miserly meal. Would Scrooge spend a little extra for a special Christmas Eve dinner? "Bah, humbug!"

Everyone is looking for that perfect gift or dish for Christmas dinner. Look for these special Christmas items.

This cake

This toy train

This goose

This pocket watch

This hat

This sled

This rocking horse

This doll

The ghost of Scrooge's former partner, Jacob Marley, has come to warn Scrooge that he must mend his miserly ways—before it's too late! Scrooge will be visited by three spirits who will try to help him learn the meaning of Christmas.

It looks like Jacob Marley brought along a few ghostly friends! Look for him and for these other spooky characters in Ebenezer Scrooge's house.

Jacob Marley

The Phantom of the Opera

Great Caesar's ghost

Doctor Spook

A ghostwriter

A Christmas goose

The Ghost of Christmas Presents

The Headless Horseman

The Ghost of Christmas Present and Scrooge have dropped in on the home of Scrooge's nephew. Perhaps the sight of all this Yuletide joy will help Scrooge find his own Christmas spirit.

Scrooge's nephew and his guests love to play games. First look for Scrooge and the Ghost of Christmas Present in this happy scene. Then find these things used in games.

Scrooge

A pair of dice

The Ghost of Christmas Present

A checkerboard

A deck of cards

A cribbage board

This blindfold

A chess set

The Ghost of Christmas Yet to Come is the last of the three spirits. It has brought Ebenezer Scrooge to see his final resting place. Let's hope the shock brings a little warmth into Scrooge's cold soul.

The spooks are having a pretty cool party in the cemetery tonight. Can you find these ghostly party things?

A noisemaker

A horn

An ornament

A bag of confetti

A Santa doll

A party hat

A corsage

A centerpiece

"**M**erry Christmas, everyone!" The three Ghosts have succeeded and Scrooge now has the true spirit of Christmas. He just can't wait to start giving away money and helping people. It's a regular Christmas parade!

Find Scrooge and these other happy characters who have decided to join in the fun.

Ebenezer Scrooge

Scrooge's nephew

Bob Cratchit

Tiny Tim

The Ghost of Christmas Past

Mrs. Cratchit

The Ghost of Christmas Present

The Ghost of Christmas Yet to Come

Go back to the streets of old London. Can you find these "newfangled" things that don't belong in an old-fashioned Christmas Eve scene?

☐ A portable stereo
☐ A computer
☐ Roller skates
☐ A TV
☐ A portable phone
☐ A pair of high-tops
☐ A blow-dryer
☐ A calculator

Scrooge's counting house is not all gloom and doom on Christmas Eve. Look for these Christmas things that have somehow found their way inside.

☐ A sprig of mistletoe
☐ A wreath
☐ A Christmas ornament
☐ A Santa hat
☐ A spool of red ribbon
☐ A wrapped present
☐ A gingerbread house
☐ A Christmas stocking

Bob Cratchit's house is the place to be on Christmas Eve. Visit Bob and friends one more time to see if you can find these "house" things.

☐ A house "breaker"
☐ A house of cards
☐ A housepainter
☐ A house arrest
☐ A house cat
☐ A house physician
☐ A "home" plate

Return to the shopping scene where people are spending a lot of money on their last-minute Christmas purchases. Can you find these things that have to do with money?

☐ A buck
☐ Dough
☐ A piggy bank
☐ A "pound"
☐ Big "Bills"
☐ A "half"penny
☐ A "penny" pincher

Ebenezer Scrooge's place is a regular haunted house on Christmas Eve! Look for these famous ghosts in his house.

☐ Beethoven with his piano
☐ George Washington
☐ Christopher Columbus with his compass
☐ Benjamin Franklin
☐ Marie Antoinette
☐ Cleopatra
☐ William Shakespeare

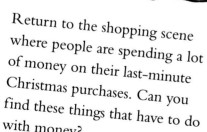